CW00867711

For Sarah Jane Phillips

BLACKIE CHILDREN'S BOOKS

Published by the Penguin Group
Penguin Books Ltd. 27 Wrights Lane, London W8 5TZ, England
Penguin Books USA Inc., 375 Hudson Street, New York, New York 10014, USA
Penguin Books Australia Ltd, Ringwood, Victoria, Australia
Penguin Books Canada Ltd, 10 Alcorn Avenue, Toronto, Ontario, Canada M4V 3B2
Penguin Books (NZ) Ltd, 182-190 Wairau Road, Auckland 10, New Zealand

Penguin Books Ltd, Registered Offices: Harmondsworth, Middlesex, England

First published 1989
This edition by arrangement with Libba Jones Associates
10 9 8 7 6 5 4 3 2

Copyright © 1989 Annie West

The moral right of the author/illustrator has been asserted

A CIP catalogue record for this book is available from the British Library

ISBN 0 216 92746 3 hbk
ISBN 0 216 92745 5 pbk

Printed in Hong Kong

BRINKWORTH BEAR'S FIRST DAY AT SCHOOL

ANNIE WEST

Blackie Children's Books

Come on Bertie,
rise and shine,
   First day at school
so be on time.

David

Emily

Hello Bertie, come
upstairs
And meet some
other little bears.

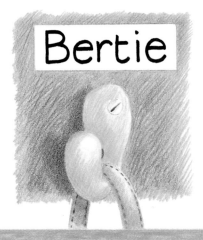

Bertie

Paint a monster
big and hairy.
Try to make it
really scary.

Clash the cymbals,
bang the drum.
   Let's make music
every one.

It's good fun on the climbing frame. Look at me. Can you do the same?

Now it's time to
read a book.
  Gather round and
take a look.

Time to put your things away,
Ready for another day.

You've had a
lovely day I see.
Would you like a
friend to tea?